THE OOZE

TASH McADAM

ORCA BOOK PUBLISHERS

Published in Canada and the United States
in 2022 by Orca Book Publishers.
orcabook.com

Library and Archives Canada Cataloguing in Publication
Title: The ooze / Tash McAdam.
Names: McAdam, Tash, author.
Description: Series statement: Orca anchor
Identifiers: Canadiana (print) 20210166669x |
Canadiana (ebook) 20210166738 | ISBN 9781459828483 (softcover) |
ISBN 9781459828490 (PDF) | ISBN 9781459828506 (EPUB)
Classification: LCC PS8625.A5582 O69 2022 | DDC jc813/.6—dc23

Library of Congress Control Number: 2021934071

Summary: In this high-interest accessible novel for teen readers,
trans teen Bran tries to uncover what is causing
everyone to start acting so violently.

Orca Book Publishers is committed to reducing the consumption of
nonrenewable resources in the production of our books. We make every
effort to use materials that support a sustainable future.

Orca Book Publishers gratefully acknowledges the support
for its publishing programs provided by the following agencies:
the Government of Canada, the Canada Council for the Arts and
the Province of British Columbia through the BC Arts Council
and the Book Publishing Tax Credit.

Design by Ella Collier
Edited by Tanya Trafford
Cover photography by Getty Images/Jasmin Merdan
Author photo by Emma Fierling

Printed and bound in Canada.

25 24 23 22 • 1 2 3 4

For Dylan

Chapter One

Bran jabs the elevator button with his elbow and waits for the doors to close. The empty recycling tubs are lighter now. They're still big, though, and he has to use both hands to hold them. The doors slide closed. Bran leans his head against the back wall. It's been a long day already. His mom got on him about his room as soon as he got home from school. Cleaning it up took ages. Then he still had to do his regular chores. He hasn't even started the English homework that's due tomorrow. Somehow he has to write a book report on a book he hasn't read. Bran taps his head against the wall.

Thunk.

The elevator shudders to a halt. The bright white lights go out. It's so dark Bran thinks maybe he's gone blind. The emergency lights flick on. A dull orange lights up the small space. Bran sighs and drops the plastic tubs. He digs into his pocket for his phone to call his mom. This is the third power outage this month.

He presses the unlock button on his phone. Nothing happens. Bran puffs out air to get his bangs out of his eyes and tries again. Nothing. Great. So now the power is down. His phone is dead. And he *still* has an English report to write. He bangs on the door a few times, without much hope. His hand starts to sting around the tenth slap. No one comes. Not even his mom. She knows he went down to the basement to take out the recycling!

Frowning, Bran sits down on the tubs and waits to be rescued.

It's about an hour before the lights come back on. The elevator makes some grumpy noises but starts to move again.

Bran kicks the recycling tubs down the hallway to his apartment. An extra-hard kick dents the outside tub. Bran curses. He does not need more trouble today. He picks up the tubs, hiding the dented side against his stomach. He kicks the door to his apartment to try to open it. It's easier than turning the knob with his hands full. No one comes.

Behind Bran a strange noise makes all the hairs on his neck stand up. *Crack, crack, crack, crack.* The noise makes him think of the raptors in *Jurassic Park*. A throaty hunting sound. Bran's not usually afraid of things. He's the one who comforts his mom when they watch *The Walking Dead*. He never jumps in scary movies. But this sound…he doesn't want to turn around and see what's making it. *There's nothing there,* he tells himself, kicking the door again, harder. He wedges the tubs against the door and fumbles for the handle. His hand is wet with sweat. There's something behind him. Something awful. He drops the tubs.

Finally he gets the apartment door open and tumbles through. He slams the door behind him. But it won't shut! The tubs are blocking the way. Something slams into the door from the other side. The door hits Bran in the face and bounces back. Bran sees a blur of fabric and skin and smells a horrible smell. It smells like death. *Crack crack crack crack crack.* The thing shoves the door hard enough to push Bran backward.

He falls over, yelling in fear. He flings out a leg and kicks the tubs clear of the doorway. The tubs ram into the legs of the thing that's trying to get in. It falls back, just for a moment. It's enough. Bran slams the door closed and rolls onto his back, gasping.

"Mom? MOM!" he yells. The thing outside thuds against the door again. Trying to get in. Trying to get to Bran. Twitching with a kind of fear he's never felt before, Bran scrambles to his feet. He looks wildly down the hallway to the main bedroom. The door is shut. His mom must just be asleep.

The apartment door shudders as the thing throws its weight against the wood. Bran tries to lock it, his fingers shaking. The sound of the metal lock clicking into place echoes through the hall. Bran almost cries with relief.

Bran tiptoes up close to the door and puts his eye to the peephole.

Chapter Two

There's nothing there. The hallway is empty and silent. Bran's breath is coming in tiny puffs. He makes an effort to slow his breathing. There's nothing there.

A flicker of movement, and then the thing is back. It presses up against Bran's door. He can see its shoulders—and its face. Its face is the worst. It's the face of

9

his neighbor, Mr. Fernandez, but it's all wrong. Mr. Fernandez always has a big smile and a hello for Bran. He's not smiling now. He's wearing a twisted expression. His mouth is open much too wide. And there is something black and gooey all over him. Bran thinks it might be blood. But then Mr. Fernandez pulls back and smashes his head into the door. His forehead splits and oozes red blood. The muck below his nose and streaking his chin is too black to be blood.

Bran squeaks and sprints for the bedroom. Behind him the door rattles on its hinges. What used to be Mr. Fernandez is trying hard to break it down.

"Mom?" Bran whispers as he opens the bedroom door. Sometimes his mom gets headaches. She often has to lie down. That must be why she didn't come to look for him. "Mom?"

He can hear the *whoosh, whoosh* sound of blood in his ears. But nothing else. He creeps forward. The blinds are drawn. The faint, cold glow of the moon streams through the pink curtains. He can see a lump in the bed. He reaches out, his hand trembling.

"Mom?"

His mom jerks forward, sitting up straight. It *is* her. Relief rushes through him so strongly that his legs give out. He crumbles to the carpet. It saves him.

The *thing* on the bed leaps for him. It gets tangled in the sheets. His mom's face, pale and gray in the dark room, crinkles and twists. She—it—tries to escape the fabric prison. Bran scuttles backward on his hands and bum. He can't think. His shoulders hit the wall. He curls up in a ball, praying for whatever this is to go away. There's a loud *thud*, then another. It's coming for him. Soon all of this, whatever it is, will be over. Bran's crying now. He's fifteen years old, and he's crying like a baby. "Mom, mommy, please," he says. He doesn't look up.

There's a hissing noise, a growl. Something thumps against his legs. Something warm and furry. "Oh no, Mom," he says. Against his legs, the broken body of his cat, Taco, twitches. The feel of the still-warm fur lights a fire in Bran's stomach. Instead of feeling cold and numb with fear, he's suddenly hot with anger.

"You killed my cat, you bastard!" he yells. He drags himself up the wall with one hand. He picks up Taco the cat with the other. The thing in the room with him sways and turns. His mom's long, auburn hair swings from side to side. There's a grimace on her face instead of a smile. The black ooze dribbling down her chin is on her neck and her T-shirt too. *Crack crack crack crack.* That horrible clicking noise is coming from the back of her throat. A bang at the door startles Bran into action.

He runs.

Mr. Fernandez is still beating on the front door. That way is blocked. Bran sprints through the small living room. He wrenches open the balcony door just as the monster who looks like his mother walks into the living room. No, not walks. Stalks. Her shoulders are up, tense around her ears. Her back is hunched. She's moving her legs like she doesn't know how to operate them. Bran yanks the door open, slips through and slams it closed. His mother thumps into it, leaving a wet, black streak on the glass. She beats her hands against the glass. Bran can't lock it from the outside, but his mom doesn't go for the handle. Mr. Fernandez didn't try the door handle either. Whatever this thing is, it doesn't understand doors.

With Taco carefully cradled in one arm, Bran looks over the railing. They're on the second floor. Usually it doesn't look very far to the ground. But right now it looks pretty far. Bran takes a breath, then climbs onto the bench. He sits down on the railing, holding Taco against his chest. He swings his legs around and grabs the bar with one hand. He wriggles down.

His foot slips, but he manages to catch himself. I should leave the cat behind, he thinks. Taco is still warm. He'd hate being carried like this. Bran would have scratches for weeks if he even tried. Tears sting his eyes and drip off his jaw. He awkwardly lowers himself by one hand. He reaches for the rail below. Thank goodness he was wearing sneakers when he went down to the basement. His T-shirt says *self-made man*. It was a present from his boyfriend when he came out. Bran drops to the ground. Thinking about Hayden makes the tears come faster. Bran slides down the balcony railing into the mud. It soaks through his jeans right away. Taco's body isn't as warm anymore. It's cold outside. There's a monster inside his mom. And inside Mr. Fernandez. Bran doesn't know what to do. He'd call 9-1-1 if his phone wasn't dead. He'd call Hayden.

Or maybe Mig, his old babysitter. He'd call someone. But he can't!

Bran's whole body shakes. He runs his fingers gently over the soft fur behind Taco's ears. He might have sat there forever if he hadn't heard them.

Not one, not two, but three shapes emerging from the darkness.

Crack crack crack crack craaaack.

Chapter Three

They're lurching down the street toward him. Their arms and legs are moving jerkily, but they're fast. Bran holds his breath and eases backward. The neighbors' balcony is raised off the ground by about three feet. A family of skunks lived under there last year. It still smells of their musty bodies. Bran wriggles feet first into the gap.

His shoulders scrape the concrete. Twigs and sticks and stones jab into his ribs. Holding Taco and squirming all the way in is impossible. He doesn't have time. Bran lays Taco down just inside the balcony's shadow. He wriggles as far back as he can. He presses himself into the darkness. He can hear shuffling, searching sounds. He doesn't dare breathe.

Bran closes his eyes. He presses his forehead to the bend of his elbow. He exhales as quietly as he can. He really needs to pee. More shuffling noises, feet dragging over the ground. That horrific *crack* noise. Growls, hisses. Inhuman sounds. Dampness soaks into his T-shirt. Hayden will be sad if it's ruined. *Hayden is probably dead.*

The thought surprises Bran. He digs his teeth into his arm to keep from screaming.

After a long time, the sounds fade away. Now there's nothing but night noises. The wind whistles through branches. Far away a car alarm is blaring. But there are no other normal city sounds. No engines revving or car horns honking. Not even sirens. If the police knew what was happening, there would be sirens. Bran stays under the balcony until he's sure there's nothing near him. Then he crawls out. His arms are scraped and muddy. His jeans are wet. He's cold in an awful, deep way.

The street looks weird. There are cars all jumbled, engines dead. Lights off. The streetlights are out. Bran's lived here on

Victoria Drive for twelve years. It's never looked as scary as it does now, in the dark. He wraps his arms around his body for warmth and looks down. "I'll come back to bury you, Taco," he says. He doesn't know if that's true. But he can't bear to just leave.

He looks up at his apartment. His mom is still pressed against the glass. She's looking out toward the mountains. Bran turns his back. He doesn't know how to help her. And whatever is happening, it's making people violent. She's much bigger than he is and stronger. Bran is on puberty blockers, but he's skinny and small. He'd planned to get on testosterone soon. His thoughts are all over the place. He remembers the sound of Mr. Fernandez's head against the door and shivers. He needs to get away from here. He runs from shadow to shadow, car to car. His heart pounds. His hands are cold and clammy. His hair is sweaty and in his face. He wishes he had a cap to keep it out of his eyes. He usually wears it in a little ponytail at the back of his head. He has no plan. But as he crosses Broadway, he realizes he's on his way to Hayden's. Just the thought of his boyfriend gives him a warm feeling. Best friends and then a seamless transition to dating. They didn't even miss a beat when Bran came out. Hayden was the first person he told. Hayden had smiled and thanked Bran for trusting him. Bran holds on to these warm thoughts as his feet hit the pavement.

"Hey!" someone says. The voice is low and quiet.

Bran skids to a halt, looking around wildly. "Hey?" he responds, as quietly as he can.

A shadow in a hedge moves, becomes people. A group of three. Two are small, smaller than Bran even. The tallest one beckons to him with frantic motions. "We thought everyone was gone," the tall one says. "I'm Mohammed. Mo."

"Bran," Bran says, reluctant to take his eyes off the street. "What's going on?"

"How the fuck would I know?" Mo says. One of the two shorter people hits him. "Ow! Sorry, Zey. I mean, how the *heck* would I know?" He grins, his teeth flashing white in the darkness. The smile vanishes quickly. He looks about seventeen. His dark hair is cropped short to his head. "These are my sisters. Zey and Aisha. Zey doesn't talk much, but she hates it when I swear."

"Hi," Bran says. He feels ridiculous saying hi like everything is normal.

"Hi," one of the two girls says. Bran assumes it's Aisha. They look to be around eleven. It's hard for Bran to tell in the dark, but they could be twins.

"Where are you headed?" Mo sounds kind of desperate. The girls are clearly very scared. Who could blame them? Bran's pretty scared himself.

"Uh, I'm going to find my…" Bran wonders for a moment if it's safe to be honest.

He has no idea what this Mohammed is like. If it's the end of the world, he decides, there's no sense going back in the closet. "...my boyfriend," he finishes.

"Mind some company?" Mo asks, rubbing his face with his hand. There's something dark and sticky on his knuckles.

"No. Not at all," Bran replies. Strength in numbers? Or, at least, company in numbers. "What's on your hand?"

Mo looks down and makes a short, strange sound. Not quite a laugh. "Oh. The... the stuff. The stuff they cough out."

"What do you mean?" Bran asks. He looks down the street. He motions for them all to start moving. He takes the lead, the girls in the middle. Mo brings up the rear.

"The black stuff. The ooze. They cough it out. My dad...he was just getting home from work. I saw someone grab him. They coughed this black stuff in his face. He just stood there, and then he started"—Mo's voice breaks—"twitching. I tried to help him. To get it off. Then the thing grabbed me. My dad said to take the girls and run. So I did. And when we looked back, he..." Mo starts crying. Bran is scared one of the things will hear him.

"My mom too," Bran says, hoping to quiet Mo. "And my neighbor. And everyone else, by the look of things."

A small hand tugs at Bran's fingers. He looks down. One of the twins points down an alley they are passing. Bran follows her finger with his eyes.

His heart starts pounding. He motions for them all to press against the closest building. He peeks around the corner, but nothing's changed.

Things. Hundreds of them.

Chapter Four

Bran pulls back from the alley entrance like he's been stung. He grabs the hand of the closest twin and starts to run. Mo follows. He could outrun them all, but he has picked up Zey. Bran has figured out a way to tell the two girls apart. Zey's hair is done in two braids. Aisha has a single ponytail. Aisha is keeping up with Bran, but her breathing is heavy. Bran can't carry her—he's too small. He can think fast though. Faster than he can run.

"This way!" he says. Mo is ahead of him now. But Bran turns off the road into an alley. He glances over a wall and then squats down. "Quick!"

Aisha realizes what he wants right away. She steps onto his knee, then his shoulder. She pushes herself over the low wall. Mo catches up. He lifts Zey over the wall. Then he scrambles over. Bran jumps after him. They huddle with their backs to the bricks, listening.

It's eerily silent. Not even the *crack, crack, crack* noise. No way of figuring out where the things are. Bran creeps to the corner of the garden. He slowly lifts his head until he can just see over the wall. From this angle the main road is still visible. And it's full. Full of figures that look almost human but aren't. Every one of them looks like they have a black beard. But Bran knows it's not hair. It's the black ooze. They're all moving down the street together. Not organized, not marching like soldiers. It's more like a high school hallway between classes. It's packed and everyone kind of knows where they're going, but there's a lot of bumping into one another. Bran watches for long enough that Mo comes over and taps his foot. Bran holds a hand up and motions for him to go back. He keeps watching.

The herd thins out. Soon there's just a few stragglers, moving slowly. Bran waits until the street is empty, then slides back down into the garden.

"There were hundreds of them," Bran tells the others. "Heading north."

"Where are they going?" Mo asks.

Bran doesn't answer for a moment. He thinks about his mom, trapped in their apartment. Has she found a way out? Is she on the street with all the others? He thinks about his dad, on a business trip in Seattle. Is he okay? Did this spread all the way there? There's no way to know.

"To the mountains?" Aisha asks, leaning against Bran. She's shivering. Awkwardly he puts his arm around her shoulder. Mo gives him a grateful look.

"Maybe. Could be heading anywhere." Bran exhales. He has an idea, but he hates it already. "Only one way to find out."

Mo understands right away. "Dude, are you going to...follow them?"

Bran shrugs. "What else can we do? Hide out until they find us? They're going somewhere. Knowing where might explain what is going on. What's happened to everyone. And if it really is..." He doesn't finish his thought. If it really is *everyone*. In the city, in the country, maybe even the whole world. If everyone is turning into monsters, what can they do? Wait to die?

"Okay. Shit. Ow—sorry, Zey." Mo rubs his arm where Zey pinched him.

"We can't follow them! They'll get us!" Aisha says, pressing harder into Bran's side.

"Oh, no, it's okay, Aisha," Bran says, stroking her hair. "You'll stay with Mo. You don't have to come with me. I'll, uh, come back and find you. When I know more about what's going on."

"No!" Aisha starts to cry.

Zey wriggles free of Mo and stands in front of Aisha. They press their foreheads together. They don't use words or signs, but it's clear they are talking to each other. Aisha stops crying. She sniffles and nods.

"Zey is right," she says. "We all have to go. You can't go on your own."

"No!" Mo says firmly. "We are not following those monsters. I have to keep you safe. We are going to hide until Bran comes back."

"What if he doesn't? When will we get food? Water? Where will we live?" Aisha doesn't sound like she was crying just a second ago. She sounds brave. She makes Bran feel more brave. "If we are all going to die anyway, I want to *do* something." She wipes her nose with the back of her hand.

Mo can tell there is no point in arguing. They spend a few minutes getting organized. Retying hair and shoelaces. Rolling up sleeves. Bran can hear Mo speaking quietly. Not to anyone, just under his breath. It sounds like a prayer. Maybe in Arabic. Whatever language it is, it sounds beautiful. Bran wishes he understood what it means. When Mo falls silent, he looks more hopeful. Less afraid. Bran's fear has been inside him so long it almost feels normal. Maybe he'll never feel unafraid again. Or happy. Just numb. He squares his shoulders and opens the garden gate.

They head out in the direction they saw the herd heading. They jog for a while, then slow down to a walk when they need a rest. They reach a main intersection.

They spot a few shadowy figures on the road ahead. They are still plodding north. Bran leads the others into a shop doorway to hide. The door is open. It swings inward behind them. Bran sees a can of soda rolling across the floor. He's suddenly reminded of how much he needs to pee. "Wait here," he says, sliding into the shop.

It's empty. Bran wasn't expecting otherwise, but it is still eerie.

He undoes his trousers and squats down to pee behind a chest freezer. It feels so good. He can't help but let out a sigh of satisfaction. With his pants still around his ankles, he shakes off and freezes. He has just pulled up his underwear when he senses something. The thing lunges. Bran squeaks and falls backward, tripped by his own pants. The thing pulls itself forward, using its elbows as leverage. Its legs are dragging behind. Its horrible gaping mouth is open, but no sound is coming out. It reaches out and grabs hold of Bran's leg.

Chapter Five

Its pale hands pull at the fabric of Bran's jeans. He screams and kicks with his free leg. The thing doesn't notice the blows. It opens its mouth wider and makes a terrible gagging noise. Bran grabs at shelves and the slippery tiled floor. Anything to stop himself from being pulled closer. The thing now starts crawling up his body.

"Bran!" Mo yells, crashing through the door. With that much noise, more of the creatures might come. But Bran can't think about that now. All he can focus on is the horrible coughing sound escaping the thing's mouth. The thing is pinning him down with its weight. Its shoulders hunch. Its head bobs. Like it's going to vomit. Bran screams again and kicks harder. Something in the thing's face breaks with a sick crunch. Its grip loosens. Bran wriggles and kicks again. Then Mo's hands are on his shoulders. He hooks his hands under Bran's armpits and yanks him out. Zey rushes up and hits the thing with a garbage can. Aisha pelts it with cans of soup. The thing recoils and disappears back into the darkness behind the shelves.

Mo helps Bran to his feet. He's breathing so fast it sounds like a dog panting. Mo stands between Bran and the girls. "It's okay—you're okay," he says, handing Bran his jeans. "Thought you might want these."

Bran turns and quickly slides back into his jeans. "Thanks for the assist," he says when he's done.

Mo snorts and pats him on the shoulder. Like a big brother.

"You too," Bran tells Aisha and Zey. "Thank you."

Zey smiles at him. Aisha nods. Zey grabs a can of soda from the shelf and pops it open. The sound is loud and makes Bran jump. Following her sister's lead, Aisha grabs a can too. So does Mo. Bran realizes he's thirsty too. He finds an iced tea. It's still cold. The rush of sugar and caffeine is the best thing ever.

They hit the road. The stragglers following the main herd are gone. In the east the sky is beginning to lighten. Bran's been out all night. He's bone-tired but energized inside. His belly keeps squeezing when he remembers his mom's face. Or Mr. Fernandez or the thing in the store. He tries not to think about what they're going to find. They have no information, no way of figuring anything out before they get there. Wherever *there* is.

They're nearing the harbor. And then he sees it. In the water. A huge, hulking black mass. There are no streetlights, so it's barely visible. But the moon reflects differently off whatever it is. It's enormous. It looks to Bran as if it goes on forever. He taps Mo on the shoulder.

Mo nods. "Yeah, man, I see it," he whispers.

Bran wants to ask what Mo thinks it is, but they have to get closer. Using cars and walls as cover, they approach carefully. When they're about two blocks from the water, they stop. The big black mass is touching the shore. It's a huge chunk of what looks like black rock. The people, the things, are walking up to it. They press themselves against it and then disappear.

"Holy shit," Bran whispers, and then flinches when Zey pinches his arm. "Do you see what I see? Are the people…going… *inside* it?"

"Looks like it. But what *is* it? Could it be a meteor?" Mo asks.

"I don't know, dude. I failed science," Bran says. He can't stop looking at it. It seems to drink in the light from around it. His stomach is no longer cramping. It doesn't seem to be there at all. He feels as if he's floating, but not in a good way. How the hell are they supposed to understand *this*? Do *anything* about this?

Zey tugs Bran's hand. Her other arm is outstretched, pointing. Bran can't see what she's looking at. A sudden flare of light makes him jump. Sparks are spurting out from a broken power line. Zey tugs his hand again, more insistently. Bran realizes what she's trying to show him.

Something's happening. Where the sparks hit the black rock, there is a flickering. Almost like a hologram. There are orange, fiery flashes too. Bits of the outside are peeling back and then reforming. The rock is being damaged—wounded—by the sparks.

Chapter Six

"Whoa," Bran says. "Do you all see that?"

"It's the electricity from the lines," Mo says. "It's doing something to the meteor."

"Maybe it's hurt by fire," Aisha suggests. "It looks like the sparks are burning it."

"But it came from space, right?" Mo says. "It had to come through the atmosphere.

It would have burned up already if it could be damaged by fire."

"I guess." Aisha bites her lip. "Or maybe it had one of those external shell things that burns up on entry. Or maybe it's reacting to our atmosphere. There's all sorts of stuff here that isn't in space."

Mo gives her a look and raises an eyebrow. "When did you get so smart?"

"We *read*," Aisha says, standing a little taller.

Bran thinks about this. "So here's an idea," he says. "Do you think maybe we can direct the power line onto the thing? Or put it in the water to electrocute it?"

Mo rubs his hand over his short hair. He looks exhausted. "I don't know, dude.

Trying to get to that line...wouldn't all those things get us? Then we'd be the same as them. It's way too close. And what about the people inside the rock?"

"What about them?" Bran knows what Mo means, but the words still tumble out. "They're done. We're it. And for all we know, there are things like this all over the world! Even if it's just here, if we don't do something now..." Bran can't finish the sentence.

Bran wishes his dad were here. He doesn't want to be standing here looking at this horrific black mass. Wondering if somehow the four of them can stop it. They're hardly the dream team, but they're all there is. They didn't see anyone else on the way here. Some people could be hiding, sure, but if they're hiding, what good are they? They'll just be found and turned into things eventually. Bran shakes his head. He needs to focus. They think the power line may be hurting the meteor, spaceship, whatever it is. But what if they're wrong? What if the power line isn't doing anything at all? Bran wishes he had binoculars so he could get a closer look.

He screws up his face. "Maybe if I creep over there, out onto one of the cargo-ship loading docks, I could see better."

Mo spins to look at him. The dawn sky gives Bran his first good look at Mo's face. He's got kind eyes and a solid, determined set to his jaw. He looks very worried. "How old are you?"

"Fifteen," Bran replies.

"Aw, man." Bran knows Mo had hoped Bran was older. He looks torn.

"You have to stay with your sisters." Bran looks out at the port. The sky is getting brighter. "It'll be light soon. You should get somewhere safe."

"Good one." Aisha frowns at him. "We'll be right here when you get back."

Zey nods too, her small face stern.

"Well, okay." Bran shuffles his feet. He wishes he was wearing real running shoes instead of the sneakers he slipped on to take out the trash. It feels like a million years ago that he was in the elevator. Worrying about his homework. Well, if the world ends, at least no one's going to expect him to turn in a book report.

Mo groans and grips Bran's shoulder lightly. "I'm glad we ran into you, Bran."

"Yeah, I feel the same way." Bran can't imagine what he would have done without them. Just feeling like he isn't alone has given him hope. If Mo, Zey and Aisha made it, there have to be more survivors, right? But before Bran can think about anything else, he has to get over to the docks.

Things are still arriving. They are coming from all over, in ones, twos, small groups. They're all heading for the black mass. It is getting crowded around the only side touching the shoreline. The things wait patiently for their turn to go inside.

Bran creeps closer. He ducks behind cars and abandoned trucks. He even hides behind a stroller. Inside is a toddler streaked with ooze. It's struggling against its strapping. Bran's heart clenches as he sees its chubby little fists waving at the sky. He swallows hard, forcing the emotions back. No time for sadness or anger or despair. Only time for action.

There's a hum in the air that gets louder the closer he gets. He can feel it in his stomach, in his teeth. He clenches his jaw, grabs the stroller and sprints for the next piece of cover. It's a good ten yards in open air. Closer to the port, the cars have been pushed aside, probably by the masses of things. There's almost nothing to hide behind except the train. It's obviously supposed to deliver goods to the port. It has its own dock. The meteor must have hit it on the way down, because it ends in a jagged break. The metal of the tracks sticks out another twenty yards. If Bran can get to the train, he can hide behind it and make his way to the closest point possible. He can even hide between train cars or get on top of them.

Determined, he looks around to make sure no things have snuck up on him. Crossing his fingers that none of them happen to look his way, he inches the stroller forward. As soon as he has a straight run to the train, he takes a last, desperate look around. Good enough. He steps out from behind the stroller.

He runs. Head down. Arms pumping. His whole body is waiting for something to jump on him and throw him to the ground. But nothing comes. He slams into the metal side of the train without even realizing he's made it.

The sound of impact echoes through the port. His arm and shoulder are in agony. Already things are turning, looking for the source of the sound.

Gritting his teeth, Bran grabs the metal ladder sticking out from the side of the train. He hauls himself upward. Only one arm is really working. The other is numb and painful in equal amounts. He has to hold on to a rung with one hand, scramble up with his feet and then let go. He grabs for the next higher rung. His fingers slip, slide, grip. He flattens himself against the side of the train and gives himself time for one deep breath. And then does it again.

He's just pulling himself onto the roof of the train when the first thing appears.

Not daring to breathe, Bran flings himself away from the edge and lies down, shaking. If that thing spotted him, it's all over.

Another huge noise breaks the silence. A metal-on-metal banging noise. Then a shout. "Hey, fuckos—ow! Sorry, Zey! HEY, you gooey, oozy, nasty excuses for alien invaders. OVER HERE!"

Oh no.

Bran edges himself to the meteor side of the train roof. His heart seizes. Standing silhouetted against a fire that surely wasn't there before is Mo. His hand is in the air, and he's got two metal pipes or something. He's beating them together. Bran can't see Aisha or Zey anywhere. The things have turned away from Bran. Drawn to the new noise, they turn toward Mo. He gives a defiant scream and starts to run.

Chapter Seven

Bran watches, horrified. The horde that had been waiting by the enormous meteor turns. The things join the chase. Mo is barely a hundred yards ahead. His legs and arms are pumping furiously. He's running down the middle of the road, flat-out sprinting. Clearly he's not trying to hide. But there's no way he'll outrun them all. Already some of the faster things are pulling ahead of the rest.

Bran rubs his hand over his face, then wriggles toward the ladder. He looks around carefully before tucking his injured arm into his hoodie pocket. It's not quite a sling, but it helps. Getting down is easier than getting up. He jumps the last few feet, wincing as his landing jars his shoulder. It kind of feels like a knife is wedged into the joint.

A soft scraping noise behind him makes him spin around. Zey and Aisha inch out of the darkness. "Mo told us to hide."

Bran bites back a hysterical laugh. "Good job."

"We didn't want to be alone." Tears well up in Aisha's eyes. Bran feels like a huge asshole.

"I'm glad you found me. Sounds like you're a whole lot smarter than I am." Bran starts walking toward the hulking, silent meteor. There's no point in hiding. He's too tired and hurt to run. If things suddenly start pouring out of it, well, so be it. He's barely staying on his feet, if he's honest.

Together the three of them walk over to the black rock. It's so huge that when Bran is close enough to make out any detail, the wall of blackness blots out his whole field of vision. The surface of the rock is smooth but not shiny. He can see now that the structure is organized, sides and angles meeting to shape an enormous rounded surface. It drinks in all the light. Aisha and Zey huddle close together a few feet behind Bran. Nothing happens. No one comes out. And so far the things that had been waiting have not returned. But it's only been a few minutes since they all turned to chase Mo. Bran's neck is tingling with nerves. The hum he could feel before has become a part of him. Calling to him. He reaches out, fingers wide. The hum increases. He leans toward the rock. He wants to touch it. He wants to touch it so badly.

"Ow! Jesus!" He leaps in the air, almost falling into the rock. The sharp pain in his hip subsides, and his mind clears. He was about to touch this people-eating rock! What an idiot! "Uh, thanks, Zey." She grins at him and makes pinchy fingers like she's going to do it again. Then she turns and points toward the power line again.

Bran shakes off the last of the urge to touch the rock and nods. "Yeah. Let's go."

They creep alongside the rock, staying in its shadow.

The electrical wire isn't sparking anymore. They wait. Bran's whole body feels itchy. "C'mon, c'mon," he whispers. But nothing happens. Nothing sparks. "Shit—ow. Sorry, Zey. It must be dead," he whispers. "God." He doesn't know what to do next. This was his whole plan. To come and see what was happening with the sparks.

A flicker of light catches his attention. He spins around. Aisha gives him a shrug. She flicks the lighter she's holding again. "Don't tell Mo I have this, okay? We aren't supposed to play with fire."

Bran swallows a giggle. "Apocalypse rules. What happens at the end of the world stays at the end of the world." He holds his hand out. Aisha passes him the lighter. It's a cheap plastic one. The kind you get at the gas station. But it could answer an important question. Was it fire or electricity that affected the rock? He lights it. "Get back, just in case." He waits for the girls to move away a few feet. Then he slowly moves the flame toward the rock. For a moment nothing happens.

Then there's a ripple, a flicker. The surface of the rock shifts and wisps away from the flame, sparkling. For a moment Bran sees *inside.* He sees the people who've gone into the rock. They're huddled in a massive pile. Their eyes are closed, like they're sleeping. He shudders in shock. The hundreds of blank faces he can see are too awful.

And then he sees a face he recognizes.

Hayden! Bran's boyfriend is one of the massed bodies. Bran would know that ridiculous hair anywhere. Hayden's mop of curly red hair is streaked with black goo. But then the flame of the lighter goes out. Hayden is lost to Bran's sight.

Instantly the rock starts to mend the hole.

"Hayden!" Bran yells. He doesn't mean to call out. Aisha squeaks in fear and grabs Bran's hand, pulling him back. Zey steams ahead, leading the way back to the train. They fling themselves into the shadows. Bran hardly dares to look back, but he has to.

Behind them the horde is returning. The things must have heard him yell. They don't seem to know where the sound came from, but they're spreading out. Then Bran sees something that makes his blood freeze. Mo. Near the front of the group, Mo is stumbling forward. Black goo is streaked down his gray T-shirt and over his face. His eyes aren't kind anymore. They're dull and empty.

Before the girls can see, Bran pushes them backward. They squeeze through the gap between train cars and creep away. Slowly they pick their way back to the street. Bran's racking his brain. *Okay, so fire hurts it somehow. We have to get fire. A lot of it. And somehow cover the meteor in it. And hope that the fire destroys it before it can take any more people.*

He's left dents in the palms of his hands with his nails. Hayden is in there. Hayden with his stupid laugh and big ears and even bigger heart. Hayden who was Bran's first best friend, first boyfriend, first kiss.

Hayden's *gone*, he tells himself. Whatever is in there isn't Hayden anymore.

The ice in his veins spreads through his whole body. Even his voice is cold. "All right, kids. We're going to learn how to make Molotov cocktails."

Chapter Eight

"What about Mo?" Aisha whispers.

Bran jerks his head to look at her, but she doesn't look upset. Or, at least, not newly upset. It is the end of the world, after all.

"He'll find us. He's probably hiding," Bran says, not looking at them.

There's a liquor store down the road, he remembers. He bought fancy gin there for his cousin's wedding. He sets off without another word, trusting the girls to follow. Or not. It doesn't matter, really. Mo would want him to take care of them, but he can't take care of anyone now. Since seeing Hayden, he feels dead inside. All he can do, maybe, is try to burn the monsters.

He's a machine. He breaks the glass window of the liquor store and climbs through. He doesn't even notice the slices in his jeans or the cut on his palm. His injured arm still hurts, but in a distant, ignorable way. He doesn't think it's broken, because he can move his fingers. Which is good. He has to move his fingers, because he has to make Molotov cocktails. A lot of them.

There's a noise outside that makes him look up. Aisha and Zey clamber through the window, much more carefully than he did. Behind them, in the street, Bran can see two empty shopping carts.

They work fast. Bran finds the strongest liquor and takes the caps off. Zey rips merchandise T-shirts into strips of cloth. Aisha arranges them carefully in the carts outside. She uses cardboard boxes to make layers.

When they get back to the port, it's empty except for the rock. No things to try and stop them now. They must all be inside. He and the girls head to the train track. It's fully light now. Bran can see the huge shape clearly for the first time.

It goes all the way across the water. It's so big, Bran doesn't know how they can possibly hope to do anything. But all he has left is this plan.

They make a human chain. Bran is on the top of the train. Zey is halfway up the ladder. She has her feet hooked around the bars. Aisha passes the first bottle to Zey. Zey places it on the train top. Bran waits until twenty bottles are lined up. And then he starts to light and throw.

The first bottle explodes in a shower of glass and liquid. Then a *whumph* of flame. It spreads over the surface quickly, running in fiery rivers down the side. The surface peels away, just like before. Bran throws and throws and throws. His bad arm hurts every time he moves, but he grits his teeth and keeps throwing. More and more of the skin withers away. He can see people inside. Soon every part of the meteor within his range is melted away. But that's it. The fire flickers, but it's dying. The skin is closing back up. All for nothing.

He stops. Exhausted. His head hanging low. He doesn't know what to do now. Wait to die? And then Bran sees something moving inside. The sun is lighting up the inside of the rock. The people are moving! Where the sun hits, the blackness inside is shivering and moving away. The people are waking up! Not as things but as regular people, blinking and confused. There are murmurs and crying. Bran redoubles his efforts, opening the same area over and over. The sun beams in. Everywhere it touches, the meteor seems to hiss and shimmer. The blackness pulls back and back. People start standing. They still look dazed. Bran can't see Hayden. Everything in him wants to go down and see if he can pull him from the rock.

"Get out! Get out!" Bran yells, his voice breaking. Some hear him and start running for the hole he's made. Bran throws and throws. He tries to hit the top of the meteor to let more sun in. He tries to keep the exit open. More and more black rock hisses and shivers away. It's disappearing into wet streaks, like the goo covering the people's faces. People rush out onto the dock. Most run away. Some stay and help, pulling more people free.

Bran has only two bottles left. The meteor isn't healing as fast anymore. Black tendrils are trying to cover the hole but flicker away in the sun. It's warmer.

Bran throws the last bottle. When it happens, it's fast. Something changes, shifts. Suddenly the whole meteor starts shivering into nothingness. It starts draining into the water. Hundreds, maybe thousands, of people are left floating on the surface of the sea. Bran falls to his knees, exhausted.

"Mo!" he hears Aisha cry.

He looks up. The twins are running through the mass of people. Mo is standing there, arms out. They both jump into his arms, almost knocking him over. Bran laughs and then starts crying.

A glimpse of bright orange splinters through his tears. He swipes his hand over his face. In front of him, Hayden pushes through the crowd of staggering people.

"That's right, just open the door, son. We've got it from here." The friendly voice of Mr. Fernandez breaks Bran out of his thoughts. Hayden squeezes his hand. Bran puts his key into the front door of his apartment and opens it.

The thing that used to be his mother throws herself through the doorway. They had made plenty of noise so she'd know they were there. Mr. Fernandez, wearing an improvised face shield, grabs her wrists. Two more of Bran's neighbors step in and take her arms. She struggles wildly. They guide her down the corridor. Down the stairs and out the front door. Into the shadow of the porch and then into the sun. The effect is immediate. She turns her face away and screams, then shivers, coughs. She folds in half and throws up.

Bran rushes forward, pulling free from Hayden. "It's okay, Mom, it's okay."

Black ooze drips out of his mother's mouth to the ground. In the sun it shivers and turns into a dusty black residue. Bran's mom looks up at him, face still streaked with it.

"Bran?" she asks, confused.

"Yeah, Mom. It's me," he replies.

Now he just has to bury his cat.

Acknowledgments

Huge thanks to my amazing editor, Tanya, who took a chance on me. My thanks also go to the entire team at Orca, who work so hard getting these much-needed books into the world. Also to the teachers and librarians who pass them to the young people who need them, and to every teen I've ever worked with. Without you I wouldn't be writing at all.

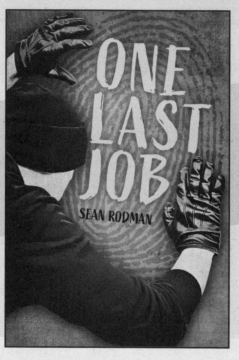

Michael's grandfather isn't your average senior citizen—he's a retired burglar with a lifetime of criminal knowledge. When a thief steals a necklace with great sentimental value, grandfather and grandson team up and try to steal it back.

"You want some pencils?" says Gramps. "I've even got pens, if that's what you're looking for."

"Don't make him mad," I hiss at Gramps. The burglar ignores us and keeps on making a mess. He dumps a bunch of files out, papers flying everywhere. Then sweeps a stack of hardcover books from their shelves. He empties kitchen cabinets. Pots and pans clatter across the linoleum.

"He's not very good at this," says Gramps.

"Shut it!" roars the burglar, not looking at us. He's busy tossing clothes out of the dresser onto the floor.

Gramps lowers his voice and leans toward me. "Seriously, this guy is an amateur. And I should know."

Gramps has lived, as he puts it, an "adventurous life." He doesn't talk much about it, and neither do my parents. But I know he had a criminal career that ended with a couple of years in prison.

"How about I save us all some time?" says Gramps to the burglar. "There's twenty bucks in a pickle jar by the door. It's for the cleaning lady. Aside from that, you're not going to find anything here. I've got nothing to hide."

The burglar slowly stands up and turns around. He pulls an old wool sock out of the dresser. There is clearly something hidden inside the sock. Reaching in, he pulls it out. A small wooden box. The burglar sneers.

"Nothing to hide, huh?" he says and tilts open the lid. Gramps swears softly. The burglar lifts up a necklace. It's a thin silver chain with a teardrop-shaped pendant dangling at the end. It catches the light and sparkles like a drop of water.

"That's no good to you," says Gramps. "Seriously, take the money. Take the TV. Whatever. But leave that, all right?"

The burglar takes several steps toward us. "Naw. I'm taking it."

"Back off!" I yell. I spring from the couch, but the burglar gives me a sharp shove in the chest, sending me to the floor.

Suddenly my grandfather's watery blue eyes turn hard and focused. His voice rattles like a rake over gravel.

"You are making a mistake, son. Leave my grandson alone. Leave the necklace where you found it. Walk away. Take the money by the door. I won't call the cops. Final offer."

The burglar leans down over Gramps. He dangles the necklace in front of the old man.

"You really trying to scare me?" He lunges at Gramps suddenly. Expecting him to flinch. Trying to frighten him. But Gramps doesn't even blink.

"No," says Gramps. "I'm just giving you fair warning. Steal that necklace, hurt my family, and you'll pay." For a moment the burglar hesitates. Then his lips curl into a sneer, and he shakes his head. Then he walks toward the front door. As he passes me lying on the floor, he swings a boot at my chest. The air whooshes out of my lungs, and I gasp for air. The burglar grabs the pickle jar by the door and then slips out the door.

It doesn't take long for me to cut the zip ties off my wrists and free Gramps. I reach for my cell phone.

"Don't do that," says Gramps. He hasn't moved from the couch since the burglar left. He's just sitting there. Rubbing his wrists. Thinking.

"Don't tell the cops," he adds. "And don't tell your parents. Don't tell anyone. We're going to handle this. You and me."

That's when Mom walks in.